the JUMBLEBEES

written and illustrated by

Rosie Pickering

For Nanna and Grandad,
whose garden inspired this story.

Little Pixie Publishing
Copyright © 2021 Rosie Pickering
All rights reserved.
ISBN: 978-1-7398396-0-4

the
JUMBLEBEES

If you're sitting in your garden
and you hear a noise that's buzzy,

and you see some little insects
that are gold and black and fuzzy,

bzz...

bzz...

with beady eyes and busy wings
and little hairy knees,
then lucky you...

you're in the presence of the Jumblebees!

Now do not be afraid of them,
they won't cause any harm,

they'll go about their business
if you stay polite and calm.

And though they look alike,
if you should take a closer peek,

you'll soon find out that every bee
is really quite unique...

There's Mumblebee...

ahem...

and Tumblebee...

BoInG!

bOoM!

BoSh!

and noisy
Bongo Drumblebee...

and hungry Tummy Rumblebee
who's always eating food.

There's Humblebee...

and Glumblebee...

and Homemade
Apple Crumblebee...

and Grumblebee
(who's often in an
irritable mood).

There's Strumblebee...

drip

Green Thumblebee...

and there goes Bubblegumblebee,
who blows the biggest bubbles
and then floats up into space!

There's Sumblebee...

and Numblebee...

and friendly Bestest Chumblebee,
who always has a big and happy
grin upon his face.

So when you're in the garden
and you hear that buzzing sound,

and you see some little Jumblebees
bumbling all around,

bzz...

bzz...

stop and get to know them
and then you will quickly see...

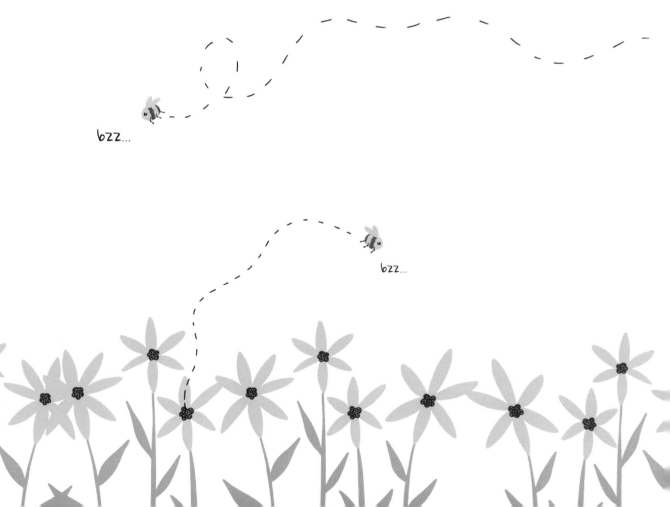

bzz...

bzz...

that every bee is different,

just the same as
you and me.

Printed in Great Britain
by Amazon

78741163R00018